OH
SUSANNAH

Books by
RUTH and RICHARD HOLBERG

Mitty and Mr. Syrup
Mitty on Mr. Syrup's Farm
Hester and Timothy
Wee Brigit O'Toole
Oh Susannah

OH SUSANNAH

BY RUTH AND RICHARD HOLBERG

Junior Books

DOUBLEDAY & COMPANY, INC.
GARDEN CITY, NEW YORK

j c₁

PRINTED IN THE UNITED STATES OF AMERICA

For
MYRTLE GOODWIN D'ASCENZO

I am indebted to CARL VITZ, *Librarian of the Minneapolis Public Library, for assistance in helping to assemble some of the material and facts for the background of this book, and to* MYRTLE D'ASCENZO *whose vivid and personal recollections made the story.*

RUTH LANGLAND HOLBERG

OH
SUSANNAH

CHAPTER I

"OH, SUSANNAH! Run quickly down to Sorensons' and tell them the Indians are coming over the hill!"

Susannah Goodwin dropped her apronful of windfall apples and turned to her mother calling from the back door. She did not stop to see how far she could kick the wormy apples she had laid to one side. Without a word she scampered down the road to the Sorensons' house, her black braids bobbing up and down.

"The Indians are coming!" she cried in the open door. "The Indians are coming over the hill! My mother saw them and sent me to warn you!"

"Oh, Susannah! All my wash is on the line," mourned Mrs. Sorenson. Then she called energetically, "Come, Yonny and Hilma, help me take the things down."

"Let me help," demanded Susannah as they all started to take down the half-dry wash and stuff it into a big basket.

Mrs. Sorenson groaned, "Oh, my—oh, my."

They lugged the basket between them and hid it in a closet off the back bedroom.

"Well, no Indian will walk off with your shirt and blankets this time," declared Susannah to Yonny, peering out the tiny window.

Hilma fanned her hot pink cheeks with her apron. "Oh, Susannah, it is a good thing you live in the last house and can warn everybody when the Indians come. You always win our races because you can run so fast."

Mrs. Sorenson slammed the closet door shut and pushed Yonny out the door, saying, "Come, run to Mrs. Parsons' down the road and tell her to put away anything the Indians might take." Yonny flew down the road making a cloud of road dust the color of cinnamon.

When Susannah got back home she found her mother smiling. Mrs. Goodwin was a small particular person who was always amazed by her black-eyed daughter's impetuous ways and bewildered by her tomboy actions.

"Thank goodness, I got my blankets in the chest," she said.

"Mother, it makes me so angry to think the Indians can take anything they like and we can't say a word about it," grumbled Susannah.

"Your father has explained to you many times that the

Indians think the whites stole their land away from them.
So they feel they have a perfect right to take anything
they fancy from us. But they never take anything really
valuable, I guess."

Susannah stood at the window watching the path from
the road.

"Here they come!" she said suddenly.

Without rapping on the door of the little frame house,

four Indians clumped in and sat down. They spoke not one word but they looked around with bright sharp eyes.

Mrs. Goodwin pretended she was busy making a new crock of yeast from potatoes. Out of the corner of her eye she saw the tallest of the Indians stand up and stare at the four loaves of bread ready to pop into the oven. They were smooth and nicely raised.

Susannah watched with a frown of disapproval. The dimple in her firm stubborn chin grew very deep, which meant that she was likely to lose her temper.

He poked a dirty finger into each loaf, leaving a deep round hole. He grunted with satisfaction.

Susannah turned around angrily. "Oh, Mother!" she whispered.

Mrs. Goodwin gave her a sharp glance of warning and quickly tucked the four loaves of bread in the oven. Soon the sweet smell of baking bread filled the little kitchen. The Indians sat motionless—waiting.

Mrs. Goodwin took out a loaf. It was crackling a little. She tapped it with her finger and it made a small crisp sound. She took out the other loaves and set them on the side of the stove.

The Indians stood up. Susannah's eyes were anxious, her mouth was watering for a hot crispy crust spread with her mother's good butter that was colored a golden shade with carrots. But each loaf was wrapped in an Indian's blanket, and silently the visitors stalked out and down Nicollet Avenue.

"I think they're mean," scolded Susannah, thumping the table with a large wooden spoon.

"Now, daughter, I can make more bread. That's nothing. But, oh, dear, if they should ever take my blankets that I brought from home, I think my heart would break."

"Why do you care so much for those old blankets?" asked Susannah.

"Because they are all I took with me when we came here to live."

A warm smile spread over her mother's face and she added, "Oh, if you could only see your grandfather's fine farm in North Tunbridge. It is so different from this wilderness of Minneapolis and this backwoods road called Nicollet Avenue. To see this town you'd never think we were living in the year of 1872."

Susannah looked up curiously. "Why did you ever come here then?"

"Your father is an expert harness maker and he can make a better living here. He has his factory, too, and an honest partner. There wasn't so much chance for him back in Vermont."

Susannah pounded the spoon on the bare table excitedly, crying, "Mother, here he comes now, and he has a string of fish for dinner!"

Her mother began to bustle about the kitchen, saying briskly, "Put that spoon away; you're making such a racket. And get the big spider ready and grease it well! It must be later than I thought."

CHAPTER II

THE NEXT MORNING Susannah trotted along to school, whistling and swinging her tin lunch pail against the tops of the dried stalks of goldenrod. Nicollet Avenue was a rough narrow road, and the dust powdered her stubby shoes.

It was all very quiet and warm.

"Wonder why this time of year is called Indian summer," she said to herself. "Wonder why I have to wear my red flannel petticoat when it really isn't cold today. I wish it was spring, when the locust trees are in bloom, and everybody changes into summer underwear. Wonder why . . ." She stopped wondering. She could hear voices on the still clear air coming from the school yard away down the road.

She started running.

9

"I don't want to be kept in at recess!" She puffed and pounded along as fast as she could, the double skirts of her cashmere woolen dress flopping up and down.

"Cling-clang! Cling-clang!"

"Oh, there's the bell. I'm . . . just . . . in . . . time!"

Miss Tollafsen, the young Swedish teacher, watched the boys and girls slide onto the long wooden benches. Susannah sat close to the front. The older boys and girls sat in back, boys on one side and girls on the other. Soon the little room was buzzing with a dozen voices telling, "Seven times one are seven. Seven times two are fourteen," and all the rest of the seven times multiplication table.

Susannah studied her lesson hard, for soon four children of her own age would stand up to recite together. They had a brand-new primer by Mr. McGuffey, and the third lesson had a picture on the page of a boy and girl wading with tiny boats in the water.

"Susannah, Johnny Sorenson, Ole Kittleson, Karin Momsen! Stand! Recite from lesson three!" The crisp orders brought them up in a jiffy.

"Năt, hăt, făn, căn." Susannah's voice was firm and sure. The others lagged a little because they were sure that if they followed Susannah, they would be correct.

Down the page they went, scuffing their copper-toed shoes on the rough floor. The recitation went on in a monotone.

"Ănn ănd Năt.

"Ănn hăs ȧ făn."

Miss Tollafsen said suddenly, her eagle eyes like blue ice, "Ole Kittleson, you are chewing something! Go to the door and get rid of it!"

Susannah's eyes followed Ole with self-righteous scorn.

"Slippery elum," informed Karin in a whisper.

"Stop whispering, Karin," scolded the teacher. "Continue the lesson. Johnny, speak up clearly now."

"Năt hăs ȧ hăt. Ănn căn făn Năt," he read from the book.

"That's all. Be seated now."

They sat down to study the next page, and the smallest children were called on to recite their ABC.

Susannah's eyes grew dreamy. Outside, the last birds to go south were singing as if they would burst their throats. The trees were all so gold and yellow that they lighted the schoolroom as if they were huge blazing lamps.

"Oh, dear, I'm so sleepy and warm," she sighed to herself.

"Susannah!" she heard breaking through her drowsiness, and she sat up straighter and blinked her black eyes.

"You may ring the bell when recess is over." Miss Tollafsen smiled at her and then dismissed the twenty pupils.

Kitty Parsons was one of the older girls, and everybody liked her very much, for she was full of fun and mischief. She always started the games at recess.

When she said "Let's play pigtails!" all the others screamed with delight.

Susannah began to unbraid her long black hair and so did the others, and then all stood in a row. Kitty began to place them in the row.

"Where shall I stand, Kitty?" cried Susannah, dancing impatiently up and down.

"Next to Karin!" Kitty shouted, pushing her into place and measuring the height of each girl, so that the tallest led down to the shortest. Giggling and pushing, they finally stood still and Kitty laughed. "Now, begin!"

Susannah divided her hair into two parts; then she reached for a strand of Karin's blonde hair and carefully divided the mixed tresses into three parts, braiding them together into a long plait. She turned to her neighbor and took a strand of her hair and did the same thing. Each girl was busy doing as she had done.

Suddenly Karin turned her head a bit too far, and Susannah yelled, "Ouch! You're pulling!"

"Ouch! Stand still!" someone else cried.

Between giggles and hair pullings, the row of seven girls, all different heights, arms linked, stood at last with their pigtails braided together.

All the other children sat on the rail fence to watch.

"March!" ordered Kitty, like a general. "Keep your heads up!"

Screams of laughter filled the air. Susannah stepped high, her black hair oddly mixed with blonde. Suddenly, Ole Kittleson sneaked up and yanked one of her braids.

"Ouch!" she cried, and turned before she thought. "Ouch!" she cried again.

Karin screeched, "Oh, you're pulling my hair!"

All the girls jerked around and cried "Ouch!" in painful tones. Susannah stubbed her toe. Down they all went in a screeching pile.

"Children! Girls! For pity's sake! Stop that racket!"

Miss Tollafsen came running out. She had been reading *Godey's Lady's Book* and enjoying the colored pictures of the new styles, when bedlam broke loose in the school yard.

Everybody had to help undo the mixed pigtails and help to smooth and braid each girl's hair the way it was supposed to be. Susannah stood up at last and glared at Ole Kittleson. She doubled up her fists and was about to pummel him when Miss Tollafsen said, "It is time for the bell!" She looked straight at Susannah with a stern glance at the red cheeks and angry black eyes.

Susannah rang the bell as loud and hard as she could, pretending she was scolding and thumping Ole. When noon came, and the tin pails were emptied of their pies, doughnuts, bread and butter, Ole Kittleson filled the drinking buckets at the well and passed Susannah close enough to splash a little water on her back.

She turned quickly and scowled at his fair skin, white stubbly hair, and china blue eyes, so innocent and bland as they returned her look.

"Ole, you're a mean old thing!" she cried. But she knew

in her secret heart that Ole really liked her, or he wouldn't
take the trouble to tease her. She was sure of it when she
found a strip of slippery elm on her desk when the afternoon session of school was called.

CHAPTER III

SEVERAL WEEKS LATER Susannah woke up one morning to find the fields covered with the first snow. It was deep and level. She dressed in a hurry and ran to the kitchen, where her mother was making buckwheat cakes for breakfast.

"Mother! We can spread the muslin today, can't we?" she burst out.

"Oh, Susannah, eat your breakfast first," said her mother. Susannah had already pulled her knitted hood from the wooden hook.

Every fall Mr. Goodwin brought a bolt of deep, creamy, unbleached muslin from town. When the snows of winter set in, it was laid under the snow. This bleached it to a pure white by spring, and then it was just right for underwear, petticoats, sheets and pillowcases.

"Come, daughter, sit down. You don't want cold pancakes, do you?" laughed her father, as he piled six smoking cakes on his plate and drenched them with golden gobs of melting butter and rivers of maple syrup.

After all the cakes were eaten, he carried the heavy bale of unbleached muslin to the field beside the house. There was a foot of fresh snow on the ground, and the sky was heavy and dark with more snow that was sure to fall before night.

Susannah helped to spread the forty yards of muslin up and down the field, stretching it neatly and putting a little snow over the edges to keep it from blowing up.

"There, Susannah," said her father as he started off to work. "It will be your duty to keep the ends covered all winter, especially in early spring when the snow begins to thaw and melt."

"I know, Father. I know the Indians would rip off as far as they could, if they should spy the tiniest edge." Her eyes snapped with determination. She made a snowball and threw it at imaginary Indians.

"Oh, Susannah, don't get your mittens wet. Come and get ready for school," her mother called from the doorway.

That walk to school was exhilarating. The fresh snow made the air seem as if it had been washed clean, and the juncos flew ahead of her on the roadside hedges with sweet chirping voices. But when she got to school, the warm air and the rosy stove were welcome.

That morning, the Indians going to town came into the schoolroom and sat around the big drum stove. They took off their boots to warm and dry their cold feet.

Miss Tollafsen's face grew red and disturbed, and her nose crinkled disdainfully, but she didn't say a word. The Indians were on their way to the center of Minneapolis to trade and buy. They drank buckets of water while they rested. They never spoke a single word.

The buckets had to be filled by Ole Kittleson, for he had the highest marks and it was his privilege. He grinned

at Susannah every time an Indian drained a bucket, and
he always passed her with a teasing flash of his blue eyes,
to which she responded with a frown of disapproval.

Lessons were recited as usual, for the children were all
accustomed to the silent visitors. Susannah noticed Karin
holding out her slate, and from the corner of her eyes she
read, "Come to my party after school?"

She took her own slate and wrote with the squeaky
slate pencil, "Yes."

"Karin!" The teacher's voice was stern. "Stand in the
corner until you remember that it is wrong to write notes
in school." Then she added, "You stay in at recess, Susannah."

Both girls felt their faces grow rosy and flustered.

Susannah stayed in. She saw the children play crack-
the-whip in the fresh snow. She saw Miss Tollafsen cross
the road and go up a path, to see why Kitty Parsons was
not at school. She tiptoed to the teacher's desk. There lay
a *Godey's Lady's Book* for the year of 1871. It was
November, just a year ago. She opened it quickly. There
were grown-up dresses, hats, fancywork ideas and new
ways to dress hair with rolls, looped plaits and long curls.

She turned the pages. There was a colored picture of
fall styles, and a little girl in a white poplin dress trimmed
with bands of red velvet, and a red plush sacque trimmed
with red velvet and a tiny red hat with a black feather.
She wore red buttoned shoes with dangling red silk tassels.
Susannah's heart stood still. The shoes were so delicate

and slender. She looked and looked, wishing for nothing in the world so much as a pair of red kid shoes with tassels.

Her own stubby laced shoes with heavy soles and scuffed toes bound with copper, her stockings with stripes of red, green and black that she had knitted herself, were not at all like those in the picture. She imagined herself stepping daintily and placing those precious shoes this way and that way.

"Susannah! What are you up to?" A voice broke in on her lovely privacy.

She looked up. Her guilty heart beat fast. Miss Tollafsen would surely keep her after school. But instead she said, "What makes your eyes so big and shiny?"

Then she looked at the magazine lying there on her desk. She saw the folded fashion sheet spread out with its colored pictures.

"Why, Susannah, it is a sweet costume, isn't it? You would look nice in it, too."

"Oh, do you think so?" Susannah took a deep breath. "But the red shoes—I wish most of all for them." Her face was earnest, and her eyes were like thoughtful black pansies.

"You couldn't climb trees with shoes like that," Miss Tollafsen said with a meaning glance. Then she reached for the bell and rang it loud. Susannah did not hear her say, half to herself, "Maybe it would be good for you to have to be careful of your shoes."

Susannah was grateful that her teacher had forgotten to

scold her, and as she slipped along the bench, her mind
was filled with visions of herself in red kid shoes with
buttons of red, and red silk tassels dangling. If she had
them, she would wear them to Karin's party that afternoon.

CHAPTER IV

KARIN MOMSEN'S FATHER was a Norwegian immigrant who had come to Minneapolis when he was just a lad. Her mother was a Yankee, so she knew how to make molasses taffy for popcorn balls, and she directed the girls in the large kitchen just how to get it started. The boys shucked and popped a big bowlful of corn. When the syrup was poured into biscuit pans, everyone sniffed and said it smelled so good. Ole Kittleson carried the pans outdoors to cool and Karin said, "Let's play *The Dusty Miller* until it is cool enough to handle."

They made a double circle, and Ole managed to get himself beside Susannah. They started singing and marching in a circle arm in arm, side by side.

25

"*There was a dusty Miller and he worked in a mill,*
And he worked all day with a right good will.
One hand in the hopper and the other in the sack,
And every time the wheel stops the boys turn back."

Dusty Miller

With marked rhythm

There was a dus-ty mil-ler and he worked in a mill, And he
worked all day with a right good will. One hand in the hop-per and the
oth-er in the sack, And ev-'ry time the wheel stops the boys turn back.

When they reached this part of the song, the boys turned and went in the opposite direction and the song was sung over. When the boys turned back the next time, they had new partners. Then the girls turned back in the next game.

Ole was singing loud and fast to try to get the song to end at the place where he would have Susannah for his partner. She was determined that she would get someone else, and as he skipped triumphantly along, she thrust out her foot and tripped him up and he stumbled ahead into the next place, nearly losing his balance. Karin screeched, "Don't be so rough, Susannah!"

The game broke up in a good-natured tussle, and Susannah was hopping about on one foot accusing Ole of having stepped on it. "Ole, you mean old thing!" she complained.

"Karin, isn't that candy ready yet?" she grumbled.

"I'll see!" She ran out and stuck a finger in each pan, and called back, "Yes. Oh, golly! It's just right!"

Susannah was determined that Ole should not be her partner for making popcorn balls, and she whispered to Karin not to let her get him. So Karin scooped up a mass of sticky syrup and popcorn, and ordered Johnny to take it to Susannah. Susannah grinned, but after she and Johnny had made half-a-dozen nicely shaped balls, they were horrified to find them uneatable.

"It's got salt in it!" wept Susannah, with angry tears falling from her black eyes. The dimple in her chin deepened. "You put salt in it when we were buttering our hands, Ole!"

She turned fiercely to the bland blue eyes of Ole.

"You—you old whitehead!" she blubbered, and rubbed her fists in her eyes.

"Oh, Susannah, don't cry," comforted Karin. "I'll never ask that Ole Kittleson to another party. You take some of my popcorn balls."

"Take some of mine, too," coaxed Kitty.

But when Susannah wrapped up her share to take home,

she found more than half of Ole's share tucked in her lunch pail. She ran back to whisper to Karin, "Ole was only teasing me. Please don't be angry with him, Karin."

"Well, I won't be if you aren't, Susannah," agreed Karin.

That evening, as Susannah sat by the lamp sewing a long seam in a new petticoat, she said suddenly, "Mother, it's almost Christmas, isn't it?"

"Why, yes, Susannah, so it is." Her mother was busy turning the heel of a sock she was knitting.

"I saw a picture of a little girl in red shoes in *Godey's Lady's Book*. She was just about my size, too." Her voice was wistful.

"Is that a hint, Susannah?" Her father looked up from the Almanac he was studying.

She blushed in confusion. "No! Well—yes, Father. I—oh, how I'd love a pair of red shoes for Christmas!"

Her mother lifted her head. "They cost a lot of money. You mustn't get your heart set on red shoes. Besides, you couldn't wear such fine shoes on these rough roads, nor climb trees and fences. Oh, dear, you are such a tomboy." She shook her head sadly.

"Now, back East . . ."

Susannah looked at her mother with a pout. Her father had stuck his nose in the Almanac and pretended he was not listening.

Susannah sighed and admitted finally: "I know, Mother, they would get scuffed so soon, and we never go to Minneapolis—well, hardly ever—where there are nice smooth wooden sidewalks. Some children go to church there and wear Sunday shoes and dresses."

Then to change the subject that seemed to make her heart ache, she coaxed, "Could I stop sewing and color pictures in last year's Almanac?"

"When you finish the seam you may."

"It is done!" shouted Susannah a while later. She jumped up and flew to get her colored crayons from last Christmas, and the old Almanac.

For the next few weeks Susannah was very busy with her Christmas plans. She could hardly wait. Christmas morning she woke early. She fumbled for her knitted slippers and ran to the fireplace where her stocking hung.

Her eyes were enormously bright and eager as she drew out an orange—a Christmas orange that would have to last days and days.

She always found one as a treat every Christmas. There was an apple and some striped stick candy smelling of peppermint and cinnamon. Walnuts made hard lumps, and something else was in the bottom at the toe. She pulled it out at last, whispering in the frosty air, "Ooooh!" and her breath made a white cloud.

"A little red heart covered with beads, all colors. It's a pincushion!" Susannah exclaimed.

She took it to the window and examined it. It was fat and hard and brightly patterned with beads, and she knew at once it was the work of the Indians. She gazed and

gazed with glowing eyes, until she began to shiver from the cold. Then she took two packages from a hiding place and laid them on the breakfast table, and crept into bed until it would be time to get up.

She could hardly wait until her father opened his package and cried, with astonishment, "Knitted wristlets! Just what I wanted!"

Her mother stared at her present and at last said, "Why, Susannah, when did you knit these, and who showed you how? They are different from any I've ever seen."

"I'm glad you like your mittens, Mother. I did them between times, and Mrs. Sorenson showed me. She says they are Swedish. Do you like the colors and patterns?"

Her mother nodded and smiled, and said the work was very well done.

"What a busy little girl you have been!" said her father. "I wish we could have bought you the red kid shoes." He hesitated a bit. But before he could say any more, Susannah jumped into his lap and hugged him hard, crying in a happy voice, "I love my pincushion, Father. And I will keep it as long as I live!"

All that winter there was so much snow that Susannah never gave a thought to the muslin that lay bleaching under it. But one day, toward the end of February, there was a sudden thaw and all the roofs had dangling dripping icicles sparkling on their eaves. The snow banks melted at the edges and ran in tiny rivulets at the side of the road. Thin ice formed on them, and everyone thought it great fun to break the "Tickly-benders" with just a tap of a shoe. It made such a tiny musical tinkle when the delicate ice broke.

The schoolroom was stuffy, and the children yawned and shifted restlessly on the hard benches. At recess Kitty said, "My mother says you may come home and slide on our hill and stay to supper."

"Oh, goody!" Susannah cried.

Kitty linked arms with her, and they strolled around while she invited four other girls and boys. They could hardly wait for school to be over. Suddenly, Susannah's heart dropped to the very bottom of her shoes. She remembered the thaw and the edges of the muslin that were

sure to be uncovered if the thaw kept up. The next morning, she knew, if any Indians passed along Nicollet Avenue, they would see where it had been laid and would tear off as far as it had thawed. It might mean the loss of yards and yards of muslin.

"Oh, Kitty! I've got to go home. I can't come and slide

because our muslin is probably uncovered at the edges
by now."

Tears stood in her black eyes and they glittered with dis-
appointment. A party was so rare, and playtime with other
children was such fun, especially if you were asked to
Kitty's house where everything was much finer than in
other homes. Susannah had to knit all her stockings and
hoods and mittens and sew seams in her petticoats, and that
took up most of her time after school. She felt as if she
were giving up the dearest pleasure of her life.

"Mean old Indians!" she scolded to herself later, while
she pushed and piled snow over the bare edges of the
muslin that showed very plainly now.

"Why should it have to thaw right now, anyway?" she
grumbled, and kicked violently at the snow.

But the next morning at recess Karin said, "Look!
There are some Indians coming down the road."

They watched them pass. One had a bundle of muslin.
They could see one end sticking out from under his
blanket. Susannah gasped.

"Karin, someone didn't cover their muslin and the
Indians took a big piece of it, yards and yards."

"Oh, Susannah!" Karin's voice was filled with anxiety.
"Maybe it is ours. I didn't cover the edges yesterday
because I thought the Indians wouldn't come. And, oh,
dear, I went sliding at Kitty's and stayed for supper until
dark. What will my mother say now?" she wailed. "We
won't have enough for spring sewing and new under-

clothes." Tears ran down her rosy cheeks as she thought of what had happened.

"Karin, don't cry, please," begged Susannah, knowing that it must have been Karin's muslin they saw the Indians carrying off, for it was the only field between her own house and the school that had muslin out to bleach.

"Maybe my mother will have some left over."

"Cling-clang! Cling-clang!" went the bell.

"There's the bell!" she warned. "Wipe your eyes."

Karin wiped her eyes and blew her nose hard. Susannah put her sturdy comforting arm around her, and the two girls went back into the schoolhouse.

CHAPTER V

"Susannah! What *are* you doing in the pantry?"

Hearing her mother's voice, Susannah slipped the cover of the firkin back, and it made a clattery noise on the small wooden bucket. She came out to meet her mother's rather stern and questioning gaze.

"Have you been eating those ginger cookies I am saving for tomorrow?"

"No, Mother," said Susannah primly. She smoothed her apron and sat down in the kitchen rocker.

"I was looking to see if we had plenty of dried beans. I thought you might let me have some if . . ." She smiled winsomely and coaxed, "There are lots of them in the firkin, and some lima and kidney beans, too."

"Dear me. And then I suppose you'll be messing around with dyes to color them, next thing," complained her mother.

The rocker creaked as Susannah rocked back and forth vigorously.

"The ground is just right now. All the boys are playing marbles, and it is time for playing beans, too. Karin's mother has some red netting she saved from a basket of peaches last summer. She said we could color our beans in her kitchen."

"Susannah!" warned her mother. "That rocker is going to bump the table if you don't stop rocking so hard."

Susannah wheedled again, "May I have some beans, Mother?"

"Well, I suppose so," said her mother. "But I never heard of that game back East—playing beans. Another thing, they never have shell beans, we always had shell beans back East."

"Oh, goody!" Susannah sprang from the rocker with such energy that it flew violently back against the table, knocking a tin cup to the floor.

"Oh, Susannah, don't fly about so! You must mend your ways. You're getting to be such a tomboy. I can't keep any order in this house."

Her mother frowned and picked up the cup. She always moved very precisely and never bumped against chairs or tables, or mussed up the rag rugs, because she didn't fly about with such energy as Susannah did.

"I'm going to make a bean bag to carry my beans in. Could I have a little snip of blue checked gingham?"

Before her mother could answer, Susannah had the scrap bag out and was rummaging in it and pulling out a small roll.

"This piece, see? It's just right for a little bag, and I'll put a drawstring in it."

"All right, then. It is a good piece for a quilt, but I guess you can have it." Her mother was looking over her shoulder.

"Look, Mother, could I have these scraps of yellow? Karin hasn't anything for yellow-colored beans." She held it up, and Mrs. Goodwin examined the scraps carefully. They were being saved for quilting, but the eager pleading eyes of her daughter were too much for her to refuse.

The next day, after school, Karin and Susannah tore away as fast as they could to Karin's house. They put a bit of red netting in a cup of warm water, and it turned to a deep lovely rose. The longer it stood the redder it became.

"Let's count our beans, so we know how many we each have before we color them," suggested Karin.

They piled the beans together. Susannah counted and announced 450 beans altogether. "How many does that make for each of us?"

"Oh, Susannah, I don't exactly know. Why don't you divide them into two piles? It will come right, then." Karin's perplexed eyes cleared up. They had never had such a big number to divide in school.

The little white beans came out all shades of red and rose and pink. Susannah had soaked her yellow scraps in warm water, and soon there were two piles of yellow beans.

"I got some blue tissue paper to make blue beans," said Karin, opening a cupboard. She stood on a chair to reach the top shelf. Susannah looked up excitedly. "Let's mix blue and red and have some purple beans!"

Karin grinned back. "And blue and yellow mixed for green beans!"

Susannah chuckled. "We'll have the most colors of anyone in school."

The next day, at recess, eight girls gathered around a hole in the smooth clayey ground the size of a porridge bowl. Susannah took a stick and scratched a ring about three feet away from the hole.

"How many do we put in?" asked Kitty Parsons, proudly swinging her new plaid gingham bean bag.

"Let's put in four each," suggested Karin.

"Don't they look pretty!" Hilma admired, as she dropped her beans in the hole. Some beans were white or brown or red, none were as gayly colored as Karin's or Susannah's.

Each girl laid her lima bean or kidney bean shooter on the line of the circle.

"We've got to count out to see who has first play," ordered Susannah. She commenced by touching each girl in turn with her finger, as she recited word by word,

"Intry, mintry, cutry-corn,

Apple seed and apple thorn.

Wire, briar, limber-lock,

Twelve geese in a flock.

Some flew east, some flew west,

Some flew over the cuckoo's nest.

One, two, three—out goes she!"

Her finger landed on Kitty. "Kitty is out!" they all shouted.

Over and over she recited until only Hilma was left. So she had first turn. She knelt before her shooter and carefully crooked her second finger and thumb against the large bean and snapped it.

"Missed!" screamed Kitty as she dropped down and took a turn. She sent her shooter almost into the hole.

It was Karin's turn. She squatted down, her blue eyes fixed on the hole full of beans. Snap! Into the hole her shooter popped. She jumped up and scooped all the beans from the hole into her bag.

"Let's play again," teased Kitty. "We've got enough time before that old bell rings."

Susannah knelt. She snapped her shooter hard. So hard that it flew over the hole to the other edge of the circle and bounced out.

"Oh, Susannah! You always do things so hard!" giggled Kitty when her turn came next. Slowly she took aim and snapped the fat white lima bean spang into the bean hole. She squealed with delight. "Now I will get some of the pretty beans Karin and Susannah have. They are the only ones with purple and yellow beans." She tumbled them into her plaid bag just as the bell rang, and with rosy cheeks and cold red fingers, they all left the bright April sunshine for the stuffy room.

Susannah yanked up her stockings that were damp and muddy from kneeling on the ground. She hung her bean bag under her coat on the wooden peg. She took a long drink of water from the bucket and hung up the tin dipper. She slipped into her seat. She looked at her desk, and a horrifying sight met her unbelieving eyes.

Her neat copy book was open, and right across her labored penmanship was sprawled a huge blot of ink. She stared speechless with dismay. No one knew how hard she had worked to have it neatly done. How could it have happened? The inkwells were all properly arranged on teacher's desk. The copy book had been carefully tucked away in her desk when she had gone out for recess.

She burst into loud sobs. Every startled eye was on her.

"Susannah!" Miss Tollafsen rose behind her desk and came forward. She saw the huge ink spot on the copy book.

"Why, Susannah, how could you be so careless?" she said.

Susannah sobbed through her salt-tasting tears, "I didn't do it."

Miss Tollafsen picked up the copy book. The ink spot fell off! She looked at it lying on the floor. It was a piece of paper, inked and cut out the shape of a big blot.

There was a snickering and giggling that stopped as soon as she looked up, stern and forbidding. She looked at each pupil. She saw the red faces and pink ears of Johnny Sorenson and Ole Kittleson. They looked as if they knew something about it. She noticed that all other eyes were turned almost unwillingly in the same direction.

"Did you do it, Johnny?" Her voice was as cold as ice.

He hung his head and muttered, "No, ma'am."

"Did you, Ole?" He refused to answer, his blue eyes bluer and more innocent than ever.

She walked across the front of the room, the pleats and ruffles of her long sweeping skirt swishing like an angry tail. She stopped and folded her hands across her waist and announced firmly, "If you don't tell who did it, we will not have a school picnic next month."

There was a complete silence in the room, with every face unhappy, worried, and miserable. Miss Tollafsen stood there as if she had a rod of iron down her back.

Finally, Ole gulped, "I did it, teacher."

A great sigh of relief went up. Feet scuffed on the floor, and Miss Tollafsen said, "Go sit in the corner, Ole, and put on the Dunce cap."

Ole scuffed along and took the tall Dunce cap from the

stool and perched it on his towhead, glowering at the
school as he climbed up and faced the wall.

Susannah felt glad that her copy book was not ruined
and very cross with Ole. But somehow the afternoon
seemed longer than usual with Ole sitting in that corner
of disgrace.

When they all started for home, Karin, Hilma, Johnny,
and Ole and Susannah, they stopped to see if there were
any pussy willows left. Karin ran ahead and dashed down
an embankment where the lush moist earth produced
enormous pussy willows, and called back, "There are
none. They have tiny leaves now."

Ole and Johnny followed her, and Johnny ran his fingers up and down the smooth young bark and said, "This
wood is just right now for whistles."

"Let's see you make one," begged Karin.

They all sat on a log except Susannah, who was not
going to speak to Ole at all. She found a branch, just high
enough to hang on and chin herself. The boys took out
their jackknives and cut slim branches of willow, about
four inches long. They dipped them again and again in
swamp water and lightly pounded the tender bark with
their knife handles until it was ready to be slipped away
from the wood, making a hollow tube.

A slanting piece was cut off the tube at one end, and a
little further along a notch was cut out like the letter V.
Then the wood inside the bark was coaxed out. The end
that had the slanting cut on it was cut off about half an

inch, and after one side had been shaved off a bit, it was put back into the hollow tube of bark. That was the end to put in the mouth, and air could pass through it to the V-shaped notch just beyond it. The remaining inside wood was poked into the other end of the whistle to block up that end.

Johnny finished his first, and he blew hard and a thin shrill whistle pierced the air.

Susannah left her branch and ran up to him, her mouth opened in a little O of admiration. She fairly purred, "Oh, Johnny, isn't it a good whistle! How smart you are!"

She had not spoken one word to Ole yet, and she pretended he was not there at all. He had his back turned and was still working. Suddenly he blew his whistle. It was not one single shrill note, but a string of notes going up high and going down low, as he pushed the long plug of wood in and out the end of the bark tube.

In one accord they gasped, "Oh, Ole! What a wonderful whistle!"

That is, all except Susannah. She jumped off a rail fence where she had perched and said, "I must hurry along home."

They all trotted along the road, with the boys whistling as loud as they could, until they came to Karin's house. Susannah did not stop, as usual, to swing on the gate. She skipped off, crying, "Good-by, see you tomorrow."

Ole's house was next. "Good-by," he called.

Susannah did not turn her head or answer. She kept her nose in the air and splashed carelessly in the muddy ditch along the road.

Then Hilma and Johnny came to their lane and said their good-bys.

All of a sudden, Ole was back. His blue eyes shone and

he swallowed hard and stuttered, "Say, Susannah, I—I'm sorry I played that trick on you."

He pushed his new whistle into her hand and was gone in a swirl of road dust. Hilma was leaning over her fence still, and envious and surprised, she called, "Why, Susannah, he gave you his whistle!"

Susannah stood and tried to blow it, but only one note came out. She was disappointed, and Johnny, watching from the lane, came out and took it away, grinning. "See, Susannah, you pull the end in and out when you blow. Ole made a longer end piece than I did, and he cut three V-shaped notches instead of one. That makes it have so many notes."

She blew again. She pulled the inside wood in and out, and the notes went high and low as she moved it. She started to go home and stopped blowing for a second to grumble, "That mean old Ole." But her eyes were dark and warm once more and filled with pride. She turned halfway and saw Ole watching her before he went in his house, and she slowly raised her hand and waved it to him. He waved back and ducked in.

CHAPTER VI

All SUMMER Susannah weeded the vege-
table patch and went to picnics with the neighbors, and
even went to see Minnehaha Falls. She sewed, and helped
to make soft soap and picked berries for jam.

Her mother was always busy, and very particular, and
wanted everything done just right. Susannah did all she
could to help. She tried to be as neat as possible, but it
was hard not to be careless as she hustled and bustled
through her work so she would have time to play.

The Indians seldom came over the hill in summer, but
one day in September two of them passed down Nicollet
Avenue before Susannah and her mother noticed them.

That very morning the Vermont homespun blankets
had been washed and hung out to dry in the warm air.

Susannah and her mother were in the shed, filling the mattress ticks with fresh corn husks.

Susannah sat back on her heels and remarked, "How good and fresh the husks smell, Mother. Especially when you turn over at night. It makes me think of summer and the evening wind making rustling noises in the cornfield."

Her mother stood up and brushed the fine dust from her dress. She had just sewed up the opening in the tick. "Take hold of that end, daughter. It is so light that we can carry it into the house together."

She stuck her needle and thread in the front of her waist, and they began to cross from the shed to the house. All of a sudden Mrs. Goodwin dropped her end.

"Oh—oh!" Her voice was loud with misery. "One of my blankets is gone!" she said.

Aghast, Susannah stared. Then she looked down the road. "There go two Indians, Mother. They took your blanket!"

Somehow, Mrs. Goodwin couldn't get over the loss of that blanket, and she treasured the one that was left more than ever. That evening when Mr. Goodwin came home and heard about it, he said, "Oh, that is too bad, Sophronia." But he was excited about something else.

"There's an election parade October 10th, and I'm going to march in it. Captain Taylor is going to carry the old flag his father took through the Battle of Pittsburgh Landing."

"Oh, I wish you could carry it, Father!" cried Susannah, her shining black eyes admiring his tall, well-set-up figure.

"O-ho! Well, sir, I am going to carry a transparency with 'Hurrah for Grant' and 'We fought and voted for Grant' and two other mottoes on it."

Her mother said, "Well, Thomas, I see by the *Tribune* that you Republicans are to walk blisters on your feet, cheer until you are hoarse, sacrifice your hat and clothes to a baptism of kerosene oil from the lamps, and then it says you should go home and have your wives give you a strong cup of tea, and you'll be all right in the morning."

She stopped and added sternly, "Don't you get oil on your new hat, Thomas. And furthermore," she drew herself up importantly, "Mrs. Parsons is driving me in her buggy to see the procession from her sister's front stoop."

"Mother! I'm going, too. I'm going to be in the parade

with Hilma and Johnny!" Susannah declared boldly.

"No, ma'am!" Her mother was firm. "You are going to stay with Mrs. Sorenson until I come home, and that will be some time before your father does. You are too young to be traipsing around nights, even if Hilma and Johnny were with you."

Susannah caught her lower lip between her teeth and tried not to cry. She thought her mother was just too particular. She wanted more than anything in the world to go. Every day at recess the others had talked about the torchlight parade. They were all busy soaking cat-tails in kerosene to carry that night. The cat-tails would burn as brightly as the metal torches filled with kerosene that made such a dashing display.

After an early supper on the evening of October 10th, Mrs. Parsons drove up to take Mrs. Goodwin to the parade. Mr. Goodwin had already left with some other men. Susannah rode along as far as Sorensons', and then she hopped over the wheel, and with sad eyes and drooping mouth, she watched them vanish in a cloud of road dust.

Mrs. Sorenson was outdoors waving to Hilma and Johnny, who were galloping far down the road with their cat-tails in their hands.

"Oh, Susannah," she said with a worried look, "I've got to go to the barn to tend a sick cow. You go in the parlor and look at the family album." Then she, too, vanished around a corner of the house.

Susannah sat on the steps and drummed noisily with her heels, before going in. She felt very much abused and resentful because she wasn't having any fun.

Suddenly she stood up. "I don't care!" she muttered angrily. "I'm going anyway!" She stamped down the steps. She started to run down the road, and she ran until her side ached, and when she got to the schoolhouse she sat on the rail fence to rest and catch her breath.

It was getting dark, and the little scratching, shuffling sounds of the dry leaves made her uneasy. She was not exactly afraid of the dark and lonesome road stretching ahead, but just the same she shivered a little, and she was not having as much fun as she thought she would have running away to join the parade.

So she told herself, "I'm going to be in the parade. I'm going to see hundreds and hundreds of men marching, and hear brass bands, and see flags waving and fireworks going off and bunting on the buildings." She drew her coat closer around her neck and slipped from the fence.

At the same time she looked back, and almost stopped breathing. There was a house on fire! She stared with eyes almost popping out. It was her own house burning up!

Quick as a flash, she leaped over the fence and ran and pulled the rope in the schoolhouse cupola that hung down to ring the bell for fires.

"Clang! Clang! Clang! CLANG!" It sounded wild and loud and terrifying. Then another bell answered it further away, and then another one still further away.

Someone heard it, and knew it was the fire alarm and re-
layed the message in that way to town, where the Volunteer Fire Department would spring into action.

Susannah started to run home. She couldn't seem to get
enough air in her lungs, and she couldn't breathe easily.
Her breath came in awful painful gasps. Her feet felt
like heavy clumps of lead. On and on she pounded. At last
she burst into her own yard. The back end of the house
was crackling with greedy flames. The heat blew like a
blast into her face. She stood helpless and wild-eyed.

"Oh," she thought, "Mother's blanket is in there!"

Without another thought she broke in the front bedroom window with a stick and scrambled over the low sill. There was the blanket folded at the foot of the bed. She snatched it off, and as she turned she spied the little red heart pincushion, and she slipped it into the pocket of her coat. She climbed up on the sill. It felt as if the flames were right behind her. She grew panicky and lost her balance, and fell headfirst with a sound of breaking, falling glass.

The next thing she knew, Mrs. Sorenson was pulling and dragging her away from the fire. Like one in a bad dream Susannah screamed, "The blanket!" and wrenched herself loose and stumbled back to it. She clutched it just in time to save it from a shower of sparks.

At that moment the Volunteer Fire Department came tearing down the road. The men were pulling the engine by a long rope, and a couple of dogs barked frantically at their heels. The hose cart was unwound, and men speedily dragged the end of the hose to the pond across the road.

Mrs. Sorenson held Susannah close, and they watched the firemen with the hand engine that was called the CATARACT with its motto, ALWAYS READY, painted on one side. The entire engine was painted in lovely pastel colors with gilt trimmings. The Captain stood on the top of it, and the men on each side of the engine pushed the long handles up and down, up and down, up and down—faster and faster and faster. This made the pump inside the engine work furiously, as it gathered the pond water into the long hose.

Beads of perspiration stood out on their foreheads as they worked the handles up and down as fast and as hard as they could. The Captain grew more and more excited, and he waved his arms and shouted to his pumpers, "Faster! Faster! Left! Right!"

Then he held his trumpet to his mouth and turned to the men holding the nozzle of the hose near the house. He shouted, "LET 'ER GO!"

They opened the nozzle of the hose, and a torrent of water gushed through, leaping higher and higher, growing stronger and stronger, as the men kept on pumping the handles up and down. The water spurted over the fire and drenched the house. Other brave men were running from the well, in a bucket brigade, and throwing water on the embers.

Susannah's teeth began to chatter, and she pulled the blanket around her. The kitchen walls fell down with a fountain of sparks, and she could see her own little bed ror a second, then it, too, was a mass of red fire. All of a sudden, the flames fluttered feebly up and then died down, and the fire was out and half a house was left standing.

The firemen pulled out what furniture they could save and stored it in the shed. The Fire Chief came puffing up to Susannah. He had a red shirt with blue collar and cuffs and white trousers with a black stripe down each leg. They were very smudged and sooty now. He took off his glittering glazed helmet and wiped the perspiration from his forehead.

"Well, young lady, you gave that alarm in a hurry. If we had not come quickly, the dry grass would have caught fire and spread down to the next house and barns with the wind going so strong in that direction tonight. Lucky thing most of us are Republicans, and we were all ready to go in the parade when the alarm rang, so we got a flying start." He patted her head and added with a smile, "Yup, you've got a cool head!"

Susannah grinned feebly at him and then crumpled into a little heap.

The next thing she knew was her mother's face bending over her. She was in a strange bed and her leg hurt dreadfully.

A solemn man with a full black beard was closing up a little satchel and saying, "She'll be all right in a few days, but I would keep her in bed. Fortunately, those cuts from the broken window glass are not very deep."

Susannah blinked her eyes. There was Mrs. Sorenson, holding a lamp in her hands. Johnny and Hilma were staring at her with grave eyes.

"Oh, Susannah!" hissed Hilma in a loud whisper. "What a brave girl you were to go in the burning house to save your mother's blanket!"

Susannah turned her head on the pillow and raised up on one elbow.

"Oh, I missed the parade and the bands and . . ." All of a sudden, she fell back.

"What is it, Susannah?" Her mother's voice was anxious.

"I . . . I . . . was going to the parade . . ." She gulped miserably. "And I got as far as the school . . ." Her voice choked on her confession. "I—I looked back and saw our house on fire!" She wept loudly.

"Now, now, daughter. We'll just forget that you were disobedient. After all, you were close enough to give the alarm in time to save a great deal of property, just because you were sitting on the fence and looked back. They say the flue in our stove was defective. We can be thankful the fire did not happen when we were all sound asleep."

She drew the quilts up around Susannah. Johnny came up bashfully and held out a souvenir of the parade for her. "I brought you a tin horn to blow." It was painted red and white, and she brushed away her tears to smile shakily. "Blow it, Johnny." She half sobbed the words.

He blew a terrific blast.

"Johnny! Stop that awful noise!" His mother bustled across the room. "Go right to bed in the haymow. The Goodwins are staying here tonight."

The Goodwins found it comfortable to stay longer than just overnight, and all the children came to tell Susannah about the torchlight parade, and she felt almost as if she had been there, too. Ole wished that he had had to stay home and could have discovered the fire and rung the fire bell. She had to tell about it over and over.

A couple of days later, after Susannah had been allowed to get up, her father made an important decision.

"We will go to Vermont for a visit with the old folks while our home is being rebuilt. They want us to come so much that they are paying the fares one way." Then he explained that his partner, Mr. Nelson, would take care of the business and oversee the building of their home. Mr. Nelson had a brother who was a carpenter and glad to get the work. It seemed as if the proper time had come to go on a visit to Vermont.

Susannah was surprised to see her mother cry with happiness. She had not shed one tear when half her house burned down. Her father had to blow his nose hard and turn his back. At last he said in his ordinary voice, "Oh, Susannah, you'll have to take your schoolbooks along and study hard to keep up with your class while you are out of school."

She pretended to pout and object, but she really did not mind, for at last she was going to see the relatives and the place where her mother had been born.

It was exciting to get ready and pack the few clothes that were saved from the fire. Mrs. Parsons drove them to the station in Minneapolis and off they went, with a noisy smoking engine puffing along the track and a bell ringing to warn people of the coming of the steam engine.

CHAPTER VII

THE TRAIN RIDE was thrilling, even if it was dusty and endless.

"I never knew there was so much country," said Susannah one day, as they opened up the big lunch basket and ate the bread that was beginning to dry up.

"Wait until you see Vermont and the mountains!" Her mother's voice was trembly, and her eyes were bright as stars. Her father, too, was getting excited as they talked for hours about the places and the people they were going to see.

Susannah was very sleepy. Sitting up three nights and riding four days had made it all seem a little blurry. But finally she came wide awake, for the last small jerky train into which they had changed was stopping at a depot. Her parents were getting ready to take all their luggage off.

"Oh," groaned Susannah, "will I ever get limber again? I'm so stiff from sitting."

Then she was being hugged and kissed in a flurry of aunts and uncles who had never set eyes on her before, and she was driven away behind two fat brown horses to a low farmhouse, set in the hills, with arched open sheds and barns all attached to each other.

Her mother and father did not get out of the carriage. They said, "You are to stay with my grandpa and grandma." Her mother added, "They are your great-grandpa and great-grandma, Susannah. Father and I will stay at the next farmhouse with my mother and father— they are your grandpa and grandma Haskins."

Susannah looked surprised. Then it was explained that driving from the depot the family decided that the Good-wins would have to be divided, so all could have the pleasure of their visit. Besides, each farmhouse had only one spare bedroom apiece.

Susannah was kissed and told to be a good girl, and off they went.

Then Susannah and her satchels were taken into the parlor bedroom by Great-grandma and Great-grandpa. There was a four-poster bed, and stiff pillow shams with embroidered verses on them done in red. She read them aloud, thinking she would show them that Minneapolis had a good school.

"I slept and dreamt that Life was Beauty."

Her voice was steady and the words precise.

"I woke and found that Life was Duty," she read from the other pillow sham.

"Do you know what that means, child?" asked her great-grandpa.

She looked up. He was tall, and had white hair that fell softly to his shoulders. She puzzled a minute. Then she admitted, "No, I guess I don't exactly know."

"Tch, tch," he clicked against his teeth. "Your moral training has been neglected, I'm afraid." He shook his head from side to side.

Susannah was almost ready to cry. She was so sleepy, and her great-grandpa made her feel as if she was somehow lacking. But her great-grandma said, "Now, Abijah, she's pretty young. There's plenty of time for you to teach her, if you think her religious education has been neglected."

And Susannah loved them both as they fussed around with her unpacking. Then she had supper, with hot johnnycake and delicious maple syrup. She went right to bed afterwards and didn't wake up until Great-grandma's hired girl, 'Tilda, woke her up, saying, "Susannah, hurry now. It's time for morning prayers."

'Tilda helped her dress and wash in the flowered china bowl. The water in the flowered pitcher was cold, but the soap smelled sweetly of white rose perfume, and the towels were large and smooth and fringed with red. She had never known such soft comfort.

Susannah was very hungry. But instead of sitting down at once to breakfast, she was placed behind her chair in the dining room, and 'Tilda and two aunties, Libby and Content, whom she had not seen last night, and three hired men, stood in back of their chairs.

Great-grandpa opened a large fat book, and then everyone got down on his knees in back of his chair. Susannah did the same, but she was puzzled. Great-grandpa read a long time in the book, and then he prayed a long time.

"Oh, my knees are hurting," she said to herself. She glanced up between the bars of the chair back and saw that

everyone had his eyes shut and his hands folded. She did
the same, but her stomach had begun to make little hungry
movements. At last, after an hour at least, the morning
prayers were ended. They sat down to breakfast, and
'Tilda went to the kitchen and brought in lots of hot porridge and cream to start off with. Steaming hot coffee was
poured in the cups, so hot that it made spangles of tears
in Susannah's eyes.

She looked around. "I wonder if their knees feel as sore
as mine," she thought, rubbing them through her dress.

After breakfast one of the aunts said, "Susannah, we
have a sewing machine now, and I think it would be nice
if we made you a new coat and perhaps a bonnet, for you
certainly need clothes after that fire, poor lamb."

Susannah's eyes were suddenly as big as saucers. "A red
coat and bonnet? Like the one in *Godey's Lady's Book?*
I saw a picture of a little girl with red kid shoes!"

"Let's look in the books. I have all the numbers ever
since it was published."

They found the picture, and Susannah whistled and
hopped about with joy.

Her aunt looked startled, and she remarked, "Whistling
girls and crowing hens always come to bad ends."

Susannah did not quite know what that meant, but she
stopped her cheerful whistling just the same.

They found a picture of a practical winter coat to make,
and they looked at the number that showed the girl with
red shoes; and Susannah told how she had wished for

some last Christmas. Aunt Libby said they could possibly be bought in Boston, and that they were very fashionable. But from the way she frowned at Susannah's jiggling feet, shod in clumsy, serviceable, heavy shoes, Susannah knew she did not think they were exactly suitable for her.

Aunt Libby rummaged in a chest and brought out enough red woolen material for a coat, and with the picture before her she began to cut out the pieces.

She basted it and fitted it, and then sewed it on the machine.

Susannah thought it was a wonderful invention, because the seams were just gobbled up and there was no hand sewing of any amount to be done. It was ready to wear in a couple of days. She put it on, and paraded up and down with its fringed cape swinging out and the velvet trimming bands gleaming in the sun. She romped up and down the path to the barns, and counted the pumpkins piled up, and looked at the heaps of squashes ready to be stored away.

She gathered up a pile of frozen apples, where the orchard began, and brought them to the driveway to be kicked vigorously in all directions.

When that was done, she climbed a fence and dropped into the yard where the turkeys were strutting about and making their peculiar sweet cries. She scuffed at the gravel, and a few small stones went bouncing in the air. All at once, a great bird that was being fattened for the holidays saw her and came at her, quick as a flash. He

beat at her with his wings and pecked with his powerful beak.

"'Tilda! Auntie!" screamed Susannah, trying to climb over the fence to get away from the painful pecks. She kicked back and screamed until Huddy Butter, the hired man, ran out of the milk shed with a fork. He struggled with the turkey, and Susannah, who was kicking with all her strength, and he received a number of her kicks on his shins. At last the turkey was driven away with the fork.

Huddy Butter brushed off the new coat, rubbed his shins and said, "Gosh, gosh, gosh almighty, but you got some force to your legs!" He led her, weeping and frightened, into the kitchen.

"For pity's sakes!" cried 'Tilda. "Your face is all scratched! What happened? Your coat—oh, your nice new coat is ripped in back!"

She washed off the scratched face with warm water and heard how the turkey had flown at Susannah.

"It's that red coat and bonnet. He doesn't like red. But what were you doing over that fence?"

Great-grandma and Aunt Libby and Aunt Content were in the kitchen now, looking at Susannah with shocked eyes. They looked at her stockings, rumpled and falling down. They looked at her shoes, all soiled and sticky from kicking frozen apples.

Aunt Libby examined the rip in the new coat and figured how she could mend it so it would not show too much.

Great-grandma said in a stern voice, "That's what happens to children growing up in that wild country. They are not civilized yet. They don't bring up their children properly."

Aunt Libby remarked, "I suppose she plays with rough boys. She whistles like a boy. We ought to keep her here where she will learn nice manners."

Susannah listened hard. She heard her aunt talking to herself about climbing fences, tearing clothes, whistling . . .

All at once, Susannah felt that she was in disgrace and that she might live forever in Vermont and not go back to Minneapolis. Her lips trembled, and she struggled hard to keep back her tears. She felt her heart grow lonesome for her playmates with their jolly noisy games.

Then 'Tilda started to set the table for the noon meal, and she asked Susannah to carry cups and saucers for her.

Susannah was very careful to pick up her feet on the rag rugs, so she would not stumble and rumple them, or bump into any furniture. When she sat at the table, she crossed her feet properly and was particular not to clatter her spoon on a dish. Great-grandma nodded approval, for she saw how hard Susannah was trying to mind her manners.

That afternoon when Great-grandma woke from her nap, she said to Susannah, "Child, can you keep a secret?"

Susannah answered, "Yes, ma'am."

Great-grandma smiled like a mischievous girl, she

thought. Then she said, "I made you some knee pads to wear at morning prayers. We find our knees get sore, and we tie them on our knees when we get up in the morning. But," and she shook her finger earnestly at Susannah, "your great-grandpa doesn't know about the knee pads. That is the secret."

"Oh, I won't tell him," promised Susannah. "Show me how to tie on the pads, please."

Great-grandma showed her how to tie them around the knees before she put on her petticoats and dress. "You take them off after breakfast," she chuckled.

After that Susannah liked the morning prayers, and she listened to the Bible readings and asked Great-grandpa many questions which he could always answer. He was ever ready to tell her stories about when he was young and when her mother was a little girl.

Afternoons when they went driving in the carriage or the double-seated cutter, after the snow came, they always went slowly when they came to the covered bridges, because Susannah said, "I like to hear the horses' hoofs on the bridge, and I like to see the sunshine coming through the crisscross openings, and it is so dark inside, and the water sounds so loud rushing under the bridge." There were at least seven covered bridges near by, and that made every drive more exciting.

Her father and mother, living in the next farmhouse with Grandma and Grandpa Haskins, were busy going to parties and church socials, sewing circles, and helping to make fruit cake for Christmas, and other jolly doings. Her father mended all the harnesses for the family.

Everyone was sewing fancy things for Christmas presents, and Susannah was learning how to knit lace. "I'm going to make enough for a petticoat for my mother," she whispered to Grandma Haskins.

"My goodness, child, it will take so much to go around a petticoat. Why not make enough for a pillow slip or two?"

As none of the Minneapolis pillowcases had been trimmed, the idea appealed to Susannah. Grandma Haskins took up her work. It was a case for spectacles, made of cardboard and covered with brown silk with embroidered initials on it.

Crocheted lamp mats, baskets for visiting cards, wall pockets, work baskets of all sorts and varieties were being trimmed with tassels, ribbons, beads and embroidery. Everybody was copying some trinket from the old numbers of *Godey's Lady's Book*. The days before Christmas were filled with secrets, and someone was always hiding her work under an apron, or skipping with flustered looks into upstairs chambers.

Susannah didn't miss her Minneapolis playmates as much as she had. She was too busy.

CHAPTER VIII

CHRISTMAS EVE all the relatives came to the big farm to have supper and to hear Great-grandpa read the Bible. Susannah listened to the Christmas story as he read it in his beautiful slow voice. It seemed as if she could see the manger and the Babe, and hear the angels singing above in the starry night sky, with the shepherds looking up.

Aunt Content went to the parlor organ and played hymns. They sang, *"Hark, the Herald Angels Sing,"* and she saw her father and mother singing. She did not know the song. She did not know a single hymn, and she had never heard the Christmas story read from the Bible before. Once in a great while they had attended a church in Minneapolis, but often they had no way to get to town.

She had known about it because her mother had told it

to her, but she had always thought of Santa Claus, for that was what she had learned in school and spoke pieces for at the Christmas program in school.

As she sat there getting sleepy, she suddenly said to herself, "I wonder if Karin knows any hymns, or if she has heard the Bible story." Then, for the first time, she was suddenly lonesome for the little house on Nicollet Avenue. She stood close to her father and said in a low voice, "When are we going back to Minneapolis, Father?"

"Sometime towards spring, perhaps in March. The carpenter has been held up by a cold wave out there."

Just then her mother came in. She was putting on her coat.

"You are all coming to Grandma Haskins' for dinner tomorrow. We shall celebrate in the old style. Good night, Susannah." And then she was gone with the others, who were singing, *"Jingle bells, jingle bells, jingle all the way; Oh what fun it is to ride in a one-horse open sleigh!"* And the sleigh bells were jingling, and the frosty air came in through the open door as they all called back, "Good night! Merry Christmas!"

No one said a word about hanging up stockings, but somehow Susannah was so interested in thinking about the Bible story, and so sleepy, that she didn't feel sorry when she drew off the long knitted stockings like a peel from her long-legged underdrawers. She hung them over the back of the chair, and was nearly asleep when 'Tilda came in to blow out the candle.

The next morning she could hardly wait until morning
prayers were over. She was so eager to see the old-
fashioned Christmas her mother had promised her. At last
they were all bundled into cutters and sleighs, after the
hired man went off in a large box-like sled, called a pung,
with the milk cans to North Tunbridge.

Susannah was squashed between wrapped-up presents,
buffalo robes, aunties and 'Tilda. They dashed, with all
bells jingling on the crisp air, down the smooth ivory
roads to the next farmhouse.

A sudden warm, steaming smell of roasting turkey, pine
boughs and mincemeat rushed to them as they opened the
door.

"Oh, how good it smells and how warm it is!" cried Susannah, stamping the snow off her feet with a great deal of noise. 'Tilda was beside her. "That's the same turkey that pecked you and tore your red coat!" She helped Susannah off with her coat as she seemed so impatient. 'Tilda thought she would rip the seams in her hurry.

When all their wraps were taken off, everyone went to the front parlor, Grandpa Haskins leading Susannah by the hand. There was a tall fir tree twinkling with ornaments and lighted candles. Festoons of glittering colored balls and tinsel were looped over the branches of dark green. A silver star was at the very top, and the fragrant needles of the tree made the room smell so good that Susannah breathed it deep into her lungs.

"Oh, a Christmas tree!" She gasped. "I never saw one like that before!" She looked around the circle of smiling faces.

Once Kitty Parsons had had a tiny tree trimmed with popcorn and links of colored paper. But this tree, that had a star touching the ceiling and branches that reached out into the room bearing a glittering enchanted array of ornaments, was like one in a fairy tale.

"You poor young one," mourned 'Tilda, who wore her best white apron for the occasion and had a great frizzled front bang, freshly curled.

Under the tree was a pile of packages. Grandpa Haskins had placed there the last batch that had just come in the

sleigh with Susannah. He began to pass them out, reading the names on them. He gave her mother a tiny package, and she opened it and found a long strip of knitted lace. "Why, Susannah! Did you make this?"

Susannah blushed and nodded. "It is enough for a pillow slip, and I'll make more for you, too!"

Susannah got a package next, and she found a large china-headed doll completely dressed and a little trunk for her wardrobe. Then came another package, and in it was a white poplin dress trimmed with red, and a red plush sacque, exactly like the dress in the *Godey's Lady's Book*. There was a petticoat, tucked and lace-edged, and some black store stockings that were smooth and thin and long.

Grandma Haskins had made her a white lawn pinafore with wide pleated ruffles and a sash to tie in back, all edged with narrow store lace. For once Susannah was too excited to speak.

Then everybody made a great fuss as Susannah's mother was told to take off a sheet draped over a good-sized mystery. When she found a sewing machine under it, everybody shouted, "Merry Christmas from the whole family!"

She turned to Susannah and whispered, "Now we won't have to work quite so hard, with this machine to help with the sewing!" Her eyes sparkled, and her cheeks were rosy.

When things quieted down a bit, Grandpa Haskins handed Susannah a package. It was the last package under the tree. All eyes were fixed on her, and she trembled a bit as she tore away the paper and found a long box. She opened it. There, in all their shining glory, lay a pair of red kid shoes.

"My goodness," she whispered, and took one out. She could hardly breathe. The faces, as she glanced around the room, looked blurred. She was almost ready to weep for joy, when 'Tilda suddenly said:

"Land sakes, Mis' Haskins, I think I smell something burning in the oven!"

Then everyone laughed and chattered, and Susannah sat on the sofa and tried on the shoes. She stood up and felt her feet, smooth and light. Then with a borrowed buttonhook she slipped each bright red button into its place. As she stepped daintily and carefully, the red silk tassels switched from side to side, and she murmured, "Oh, they are so soft and light!"

"They will look nice with your new dress. You'll be quite a little lady," said Great-grandma.

Susannah kissed her and was surprised to feel how very soft her cheek was, and she whispered, "You feel as soft as my red shoes, and I'll try to be a little lady."

Then dinner was ready and everyone ate. Susannah had never seen so much food on a table, and she leaned over to call to her mother, "This is the nicest Christmas I ever had, but I wish Karin and Kitty and the others—and Ole, too—were here."

"It won't be long before you see them, daughter. Have you written a letter to Karin or anyone yet?"

"No, but I surely will tomorrow," she promised. And then she remembered how her aunt Libby had thought they ought to keep her and bring her up properly, and she wanted very much to write a letter to Karin to ask for news about her playmates.

The next day Susannah sat chewing her pencil, with a sheet of letter paper before her. "Great-grandpa, please tell me how many cows you have. I'm writing to Karin Momsen, and I want to tell her about the farm."

He stopped rocking his chair and said, "Well, sir, we got twenty-five cows, a flock of sheep and a pen of pigs."

"Oh, wait till I write it down." She scribbled hard and fast.

"How big is the farm?" she mumbled, trying to figure out how to spell "flock."

"Three hundred and sixty acres, some wood lots, but mostly fields. Don't forget the ducks, turkeys, and Plymouth Rocks," he added.

"Oh, dear, wait. I can't spell all those words, right away. I have to figure them out," she complained to the old man, who was looking at her over his spectacles with a teasing twinkle. "I thought your aunt Content was drilling you in your school work, and that your spelling was improving? I don't think you learned much in that Minneapolis school."

Susannah hurried on with her letter. "Now it's finished." She licked the envelope, sealed it and wrote, "Miss

Karin Momsen, Nicollet Avenue, Minneapolis, Minnesota."

"Don't you want to stay here and live with us, Susannah?" asked Great-grandpa, as he rocked to and fro in the sunny sitting-room window.

She looked up. She loved the great-grandparents, the aunties and everyone. The great spreading farmhouse, and the snow-covered mountains, and 'Tilda in the kitchen, made her heart feel warm and cosy.

Slowly and seriously she answered, "I would rather live in Minneapolis with Mother and Father and the new sewing machine . . . and Karin and Kitty and Ole and school with the Indians coming in even if they did take things." She drew a deep breath and said in a rush of words, "And I want to show Karin and Kitty my new shoes!"

Her great-grandpa laughed and laughed until he had to take off his spectacles and wipe them dry. At last he managed to say, "Well, it seems to me I've been hearing things about keeping you here. But if you feel that way about the uncivilized Middle West, I don't know."

All at once Susannah untwisted her legs from the chair and sat properly and soberly, looking at her great-grandpa. But he was falling asleep in his chair and didn't notice how ladylike she was trying to be.

CHAPTER IX

"MERCY SAKES!" said 'Tilda one morning, several weeks later, to Great-grandma Goodwin. "That young one hasn't enough to do."

Susannah sat in the big kitchen in a rush-bottomed chair, playing with Tabby, the striped cat. The cat would rush across the clean white maple floor and slide onto a braided rug. Susannah's giggling and hilarious laughing would make her roll over on the floor, clutch the rug with all claws, and kick and chew the soft edge of the rug. She would roll her eyes around for more applause, and then jump into the air with all legs straight out.

"Them rugs will be chewed to pieces," objected 'Tilda.

Great-grandma Goodwin was holding her specs over the spout of the steaming tea kettle. Then she polished them dry with a corner of her clean checked apron. She put them on and looked through them at Susannah, thoughtfully.

"Put on your hug-me-tight and run up into the attic and bring down a string of dried apples. You can reach the lowest strings on the rafters," she said in her sweet mild voice.

"All right!" cried Susannah, jumping up eagerly and upsetting her chair at the same time.

"But don't dawdle, it's powerful cold up there," said 'Tilda briskly.

Susannah found it very cold, and in no time her teeth chattered as she peered here and there. She reached for a string of some dried little nubbins that were the only things she saw hung from the rafters on strings, and she scampered down the narrow steep steps and slammed the attic door. With all speed, she clattered down from the chilly upper floor into the warm kitchen.

"Now, Susannah, take them off the strings and put them to soak in enough water to cover them."

She could hardly believe that the dried-up nubbins were really apples, and Great-grandma explained that they were Tolman Sweets, gathered in the fall. They had spent a couple of evenings peeling and quartering them.

'Tilda interrupted, saying, "Your aunts and I threaded them with darning needles on white strings."

Susannah's mouth was like a little red letter O, and she held the pan of apples in her arms absently, until she was told to put it on the back of the stove. She tried not to

splash, but some drops did fall on the hot stove and hissed
and sizzled and steamed.

'Tilda continued: "By bedtime, we'd have yards and
yards of apples hanging over the stove to dry. Mis' Goodwin, she covered them with white muslin to keep them
clean. Most folks don't mind a little dust, but she is particular."

Susannah thought her mother was particular, too. She
looked up, thinking how jolly it must have been with
strings of apples drying and smelling sweetly over the hot
stove, and she asked how long they had to hang there.

"Oh, a week, I guess," mumbled 'Tilda, disappearing
into the icy buttery to bring out a pitcher of milk to put
into the Indian meal pudding she was making.

All day Susannah kept peeking into the large pan of
apples, and toward supper time she could see a change.
They were almost like real apples. She teased 'Tilda to
tell her what she was going to do with them, but 'Tilda
only told her to wait and see, and nodded as if she had a
good joke up her sleeve.

After breakfast the next morning, she smiled mysteri-
ously and said, "Want to help me?"

"Oh, yes!" shouted Susannah.

'Tilda led her to the stove. "See them apples? They been
cooking for two hours."

Susannah looked. "Oh, it is a dark brown sauce now!"

'Tilda said, "You go in the buttery and bring out a cup
of sugar. I think that's about right for a quart of apples.
And bring the nutmeg grater, too."

"My, but it's cold," said Susannah, scooping up a cup of sugar from the barrel. She hunted for the nutmeg grater and found it next to the coffee mill, and she came out hugging herself to keep warm.

"Stir in the sugar and grate a little nutmeg into it," ordered 'Tilda.

Susannah rubbed the little brown nut up and down the slender grater, and sniffed its spicy fragrance and stirred it in the apple sauce.

'Tilda was muttering, "Two and a half cups of flour, salt, rising powder and a dab of sugar . . ." Then louder, "Get me a chunk of butter the size of a duck's egg."

"How big is that?" Susannah had a puzzled scowl.

"Some bigger than a hen's egg. Land sakes!" scoffed 'Tilda, vigorously beating two eggs.

"Don't lean on the table and get all floury," she continued to scold good-naturedly.

"I wish I could use the rolling pin," coaxed Susannah, as she saw the dough lightly dumped onto the floured board.

"Humph, fine mess you'd make of it. Takes an experienced hand to do this." 'Tilda was taking little pieces of the dough and rolling them into circles the size of a butter plate. She looked at Susannah and said, "Now you put just two tablespoons of the sauce spang in the middle of each circle."

As soon as that was done, 'Tilda moistened the edges of dough with water and folded them over, firmly pressing the edges together.

Susannah licked the spoon and thought it wonderfully good apple sauce.

'Tilda trotted briskly to the stove. "Wait now, let me see if my kettle of fat is hot."

"My, my!" was all Susannah could say, as 'Tilda dropped the folded circles of dough into the hot fat with a loud sputtering. She watched with fascinated eyes.

"They are getting brown, 'Tilda!" she cried in alarm.

"Don't you get your nose too close to that fat," said 'Tilda, turning over the browned sides, "or you'll get spattered and burned."

Then she took out the brown half circles with a wire ladle.

"There's your fried pies for you!" she announced triumphantly, piling one after another on a big platter.

"Fried pies?" questioned Susannah.

"Yes sirree!" bragged 'Tilda. "There's no better fried pies in the state of Vermont than these, if I do say it myself as shouldn't."

Susannah's mouth was watering, and she ventured to say, "When do we eat them?"

"Dinner," said 'Tilda severely.

Susannah's face grew long and her eyes clouded over.

"Humph!" snorted 'Tilda. "If you feel that way about it, I guess you might as well have one right now. Don't mind if I try one myself—seeing it's a long time to dinner."

Susannah bit into the crunchy, flaky crust and the warm apple sauce oozed out. "Um, um," she managed to stutter through the delicious mouthful.

When she had finished the last crumb, she sighed and said, "I wish Karin had a fried pie, too."

"Who is Karin?" asked 'Tilda.

"She is my best friend in Minneapolis. We have lots of fun playing together, and we're in the same reader at school, too."

'Tilda looked at her speculatively and said slowly, "My goodness, what you need is someone to play with. You're the only young one in the family, poor lamb. It's mighty quiet for you here. Now let me see . . ."

Susannah looked up eagerly, but all she met was a sage nodding of 'Tilda's head and a promise of something to happen the next day.

CHAPTER X

THE NEXT AFTERNOON 'Tilda told Susannah to put on her coat and hat. 'Tilda herself was dressed up in her second-best black alpaca, made with a polonaise that billowed out in back over her best bustle. She perched a small bonnet over her frizz and tied it under her determined chin, and like a full-sailed boat she skimmed into Susannah's room.

"I'm taking you to see Em'ly Wells down the rud. Mis' Wells has got a crochet pattern I want to copy, so get your arctics on and bundle up good."

The snowy road was packed smooth and hard, but on each side high banks of snow covered the rail fences and buried the hedges.

Em'ly Wells was still at school when they got there, and Mrs. Wells brought Susannah the family album to look at while she waited. She sat on the slippery horsehair sofa and looked at all the photographs and tintypes of the Wells family, and wondered if Em'ly looked like any of them.

Just then Em'ly came home, and for a while she was tongue-tied with pleasure to see a little girl who had come all the way from Minnesota on a train, and who had saved her mother's blanket from a burning house.

Susannah liked Em'ly's red curls tied with a blue ribbon. She liked her greenish hazel eyes and freckled nose and quiet ways.

"I'll show you my thimble dolls," said Em'ly shyly. "I got more than any other girl."

Susannah's black eyes were all questions. "I never saw a thimble doll!" she cried in astonishment.

"I keep them in a soap box because it smells so sweet," said Em'ly, opening a brightly colored cardboard soap box. She explained that once her mother had four cakes of perfumed soap given her, and after it was used up she gave the box to Em'ly for a birthday present, and the scent lasted for years and years.

She carefully lifted the cover, and Susannah stared. There were five thimbles dressed in wee skirts, one over the other. A narrow bit of baby ribbon tied around made the waistline. Em'ly lifted one out, declaring, "This one has a jacket, too!"

Susannah took it in her hands. She hardly knew what to say. It wasn't like any doll she had ever seen, but some-

how she liked it and its tiny size. It lay in the palm of her hand, and Em'ly took it from her, saying, "See, Susannah. I put them on my fingers like this and they nod to each other." She took one from the box and they nodded to each other.

Susannah giggled. "Oh, Em'ly, may I do that, too?"

For quite a while they played with the thimble dolls, making up all sorts of things for them to do. Susannah determined to make some to take home with her, and Em'ly said it took such tiny scraps to dress them that anyone would be glad to let her rummage in the scrap bag.

"If Great-grandma will give me a thimble. I have one of my own, but it is so small," Susannah worried. But

Em'ly said, "Yours will make a baby thimble doll. You could make a long dress for it."

Susannah laughed, and Em'ly crinkled up her nose and joined her, pleased to think she had a new idea for baby thimble dolls.

"Mercy sakes! What gigglers!" said 'Tilda, turning to see what all the laughing was about. "We got to go home right this minute. It's later than I thought."

They bundled up and made plans to come again; and Susannah looked back twice to see Em'ly's red curls and freckled nose at the window.

In early March a letter came to Mr. Goodwin from his partner, telling him that the house in Minneapolis was all ready for his return. It took several days for the Goodwins to get packed, as they all had new clothes and many contributions of furniture and bedding from the two farmhouses to take back with them.

Susannah was hunting for a small box to carry her thimble dolls in, and she passed the parlor door where the family was sitting and talking. She heard her name and stopped to see if she were being spoken to, but as the voices went on she knew that they were talking about her and that they did not know she was outside the door.

Aunt Libby and Aunt Content were saying that they wanted to keep Susannah. She would get over her tomboy ways much quicker here than in the West, where everything was so new and uncivilized, they said.

Susannah could hardly breathe for a minute. Maybe

she would be left there, so they could train her to be a well-behaved little lady who wouldn't tear her clothes climbing fences and trees, who wouldn't exchange playful blows with the boys, or whistle loud and shrill, or kick pebbles when she walked on the road.

She went to her bedroom and put the thimble dolls on the bureau. She waited until her father and mother came out of the parlor.

Slowly and solemnly Susannah went to them.

"If I give back my red shoes"—she choked down a sob—"will you take me back to Minneapolis with you? I promise not to be a tomboy and tear my clothes. Please take me with you!"

All at once her tears would not stay back, and her dimpled chin trembled and the flood of tears drenched her cheeks.

The relatives stood around all talking at once. Finally, Great-grandma said, when the hubbub began to quiet down, "Oh, Susannah, I think we have forgotten just how it is to be a lively little girl. Of course you are going back with your father and mother. And of course you are taking your red shoes with you."

Susannah's mother was wiping the tears from her hot face. Her father was smiling at her and saying, "I need your help, daughter. I couldn't get along without you, and"—he leaned down and whispered—"I don't care if you are a tomboy!"

No one else heard what he said, and Susannah began to

smile because she had a secret with her father. Aunt Libby
found an empty spool box, and she packed her thimble
dolls in it with some pretty scraps to give Karin.

At last it was time to leave Vermont. The train was
waiting, and the tearful farewells had been said, and hand-
kerchiefs had been waved until no one could be seen from
the train window.

Towards the end of the trip back home, they began to
talk about Minneapolis. Susannah's mother was counting
in her mind the sheets and new store blankets her people
had given her that were packed in the baggage car.

"It makes me happy to bring these things with me. It
helps to make me feel closer to them all in Vermont,
somehow," she said.

Susannah thought and thought about that. Finally, her
mother said, "A penny for your thoughts, daughter."

She looked up soberly, her eyes like black pansies, and
she tried to put her thoughts into words. "Mother, I was
thinking about what you said. Of course I have all the
pretty things they gave me to keep me close to my great-
grandpa and great-grandma and 'Tilda and the aunties.
But I was thinking that I have something inside me to
bring back."

Her father and mother looked at her steadily. "Yes, go
on, daughter," her father urged.

"Well, I was thinking about Great-grandpa and the
Christmas story he read from the Bible. I wish my play-
mates could hear him. Would you read it for them,
Father?"

He nodded slowly that he would, and turning to her mother he said, "There are many such things we have forgotten or expected other people in our neighborhood to do, Sophronia."

"Yes, Thomas, I agree with you. I'll start a group of children in our own home Sundays, so that they can hear the Bible read aloud. I think some of them go a long distance to church once in a while, but we can make it easy for the children. I'm sure we could use the school-house, as they do in Vermont for evening singing societies. Our neighbors come from all over, even Europe—especially the Scandinavians. If they get acquainted with each other singing or sewing together, I think we can all give each other an exchange of ideas."

"Oh, what fun!" Susannah's eyes were dancing. "You were having such fun in Vermont and now you will in Minneapolis!"

"The sewing machine will give me more time, too." Mrs. Goodwin turned to look out the train window, and the flat Minnesota lands with their faint spring coloring made her say, "I'm glad to live out here in this new country with so many things to be started and begun from the beginning—even if the folks think it is uncivilized."

"Oh!" Susannah bounced up and down in her seat as the train began to come to a jerky stop at a tiny station along the way.

"I told Em'ly Wells something she didn't know about jumping rope, with two ropes going at the same time. We

call it Double Dutch, and the Schoonmaker girls showed
us how to do it one day at recess. I told Em'ly we always
say, 'Pepper, salt, mustard, cider, vinegar, vinegar,
vinegar!' And jump as fast as we can!"

"Oh, Susannah!" said her mother, and she looked at
the red kid shoes that Susannah was wearing home.

"But I'm not going to jump in my red shoes!" cried
Susannah. And the other passengers had to join her father
when he laughed because the other passengers had heard
all about the shoes, and they knew that Susannah was going to take good care of them and wear them only when
she was dressed up like a little lady who was minding her
manners. They all knew how happy she was that Great-
grandma Goodwin had decided that she should go back
to live in Minneapolis.